# 11 DATES

## OCTAVIA JENSEN

# Content Warning

Please note, that in addition to the kinks Briella and Harrison have already explored on-page, this book also contains one brief scene involving a lactation kink. Nothing else should be new here, but you'll see the return of their light sadomasochism, public sex, Dom/sub dynamics, breeding kink, and one very territorial hero.

This book also contains multiple pregnancies, and is the conclusion to Harrison Stag and Briella Lewis' story. It should not be read as a standalone.

# The Tour Date

To say that I was happy would be an understatement. The man Harrison had become was so different from the one who'd tossed huge workloads on my desk without a 'thank you' that it was like night and day. Instead of files, he tossed me on the desk and ate me like I was his lunch.

It was everything I'd yearned for.

He was everything I'd yearned for.

I still got butterflies when we went on dates, still got them when he'd take my hand in public and I was the one hanging off his arm. Every time I looked at him, he looked more handsome than the last, and because of that… sometimes I struggled to look away. "I'm excited for the concert tonight, but sometimes I swear I could make a night of just staring at your gorgeous face."

The restaurant was quiet and dark, casting his face in shadow as he smirked slightly and pushed my glass of wine closer to me. "Could you?"

I took a sip before I responded, my red lipstick leaving a print on the glass. "Yes. It's a good face."

"And you've been a good girl today," he said fondly. "Almost like you're trying to butter me up."

"Have I?" I batted my eyelashes and slipped off my heel, then slid my foot up between his legs. "You're so hot when you're buttered up, Sir."

He chuckled, shaking his head slightly as he reached under the table to grip my ankle. "That was one time, Briella. I didn't feel clean for a week after that scene, and we ruined the sheets."

"Not the first sheets we've ruined… I don't think it will be the last."

Not smiling was a job in itself, especially when I tried to toe at his crotch and he adopted his signature grumpy look. "Briella. Don't be a brat. We have a long night ahead of us, you know."

I did know, but I also knew he was hard under those slacks for me.

It made holding myself back harder, but I was playing a long game here. Concert sex was on my bucket list. "Yes, Sir. Such a long, hard, wet night ahead."

It didn't make sense, but I didn't need it to. It was clear by the way his eyes darkened that I'd got my point across, but Harrison had some plans of his own I hadn't accounted for.

"Spread your legs."

I bit my lip as I complied, my gaze not wavering in the slightest. "Will you make me wait?"

His eyes flicked to the table as he sat back and put his feet on my seat, pinning my thighs apart. "Yes, I'm going to make you wait. But since it seems that I'm on a date with my good little whore and not my girlfriend, we're going to play a little game. Tell me your top three scenes we've done, and exactly how hard you came each time."

My attempt to clench at his words was stopped short. "Fuck me," I muttered, clearing my throat before continuing. "I loved the scene we did when you chained me to the ceiling. Coming that time was... mind-altering."

"I remember. You squirted," he commented, taking a slow bite of his food. "Two more."

"Do you remember the time we played that game where you tried to make me come and I had to fight it?"

He tilted his head, nudging his feet a little to spread me open further. "Which time?"

I chuckled. "The first time, Sir. The time when I almost passed out when I gave in." I shivered. "And then there was the time we role played at that work party. When we didn't even make it to a room and you took me in the hallway."

"Are those your three?"

Picking only three out of all the scenes we'd done was hard, but I knew he didn't want me being indecisive. "Yes, Sir. But I love all our scenes."

Harrison pulled out his phone and shot off a text, then took another bite. "Are you wet, Briella? Are you ruining the vinyl you're sitting on?"

"Yes," I gasped, grabbing my wine for a long sip.

"Such a beautiful little whore," he whispered. "My beautiful Briella. Now eat your dinner."

His legs dropped, leaving me longing for more and desperate to please him. I forced myself to focus on my food and not the sex we'd be having later, pleased with how delicious the meal ended up being, and when I finished I couldn't stop smiling. "Thank you for dinner, Harrison. I love going on dates with you."

"So do I," he admitted softly. "But we should get going if we want to get backstage. After a certain point, the whole place will be crawling with people trying to get to the twins. Are you finished?"

"Yeah, I'm done." I wiped off my face with my napkin and took one last drink of water. "How crazy are their fans?"

"You've met my brothers. Take a moment to think about the type of people they'd attract, then answer your own question."

I couldn't help but laugh as he paid the bill, and when he was leading me back to our car, I found that I was pretty damn excited. "Feel like I should have painted my nails black, at least."

"Just be glad that I didn't. They may be my younger brothers, but they physically held me down for their first gig and painted mine black. It ended up all over my hand, but… anyway. I kind of liked it," he admitted. "Believe it or not, I had long hair that covered my eyes back in the day, too."

"Photos or it didn't happen," I rushed out. "I need this proof, because the visual alone…"

I laughed, leaning in for a kiss that he denied me. "Fine. You want proof?" He fished out his phone and scrolled for a while, then handed it over.

There was a whole video of the scene playing out with Ethan laughing behind the camera, and I felt my heart flutter in my chest. He looked younger — especially with the hair — but he also looked exactly like he did now, adorable scowl and all. "I think I just fell more in love with you. Glad I wasn't the only one here that had an emo phase."

"Were you even alive back then if you didn't?" he quipped, tucking his phone away and opening the car door for me. "It wouldn't have been as bad for me, but all three of my brothers are bigger. The twins were taller than me by the time they turned fourteen, so I got tag-teamed a lot."

Once he joined me in the car, I reached over to take his hand and kiss his knuckles. "Bet you can still kick their asses one on one."

"Mmm." He bit his lip as he started driving, falling into silence and allowing me time to just stare at him. The restaurant wasn't far from the concert hall though, so he was opening my door again to let me out only a few minutes later. "Are you sure you're ready for this, kitten?" he asked. "Last chance to back out and go home."

"No, you've kept me away from their concerts long enough and since Quentin started school, who knows how long I'll have to experience it. I'm ready."

Harrison sighed in resignation and made a call, having a clipped conversation before guiding me by the small of my back around the building. "Q's going to let us in here."

## JENSEN

It looked as shady as you'd expect it to look, but unlike most shady alleyways, this one had some amazing art along the walls. The whole endeavor had me feeling twenty-one all over again. "How much time do we have?" I asked, reaching out to palm him and kiss along his jaw.

"Not enough," he growled, spinning me and pinning me face-first against the brick wall. His hand slipped up my dress as his teeth caught my earlobe, and I gasped as he slid my panties to the side and shoved two fingers into me. "Being a bad girl already, Briella."

"Am I?" I whispered sharply. "Maybe you should spank me?"

His response was abruptly cut off by Quentin shoving open the metal door, and when he saw the state of us, he raised his eyebrows and stayed put. "Don't mind me. Carry on."

"Fuck off, Q." Harrison withdrew quickly and fixed my dress for me, then eyed his younger brother. "Why are you dressed like the love child of Marilyn Manson and Gerard Way?"

"Because it gets me laid. Why are you dressed like a lawyer at a concert?"

I bit back a laugh as Harrison raised an eyebrow. "Because it gets me laid."

"She'd fuck you in a paper bag, doesn't count. Hey, Bri."

He gave me a one-armed hug, booze, pot, and cologne filling my nostrils as my face pressed to his chest. Quentin and Roman were identical twins, but the moment I met them in person, it was easy to tell them apart. Though both had soft, messy brown hair and green eyes, Quentin's were filled with challenge and mischief where Roman's were full of secrets and strength. Both were covered in tattoos from their necks to their fingers, but where some of Q's were colored, all of Roman's were black. And those things were just on the surface, their personalities differed even more. "He's not wrong, Harrison. I would fuck you in a paper bag."

"Better paper than plastic," he said, guiding me inside to the area backstage. "How soon until your entourage descends, Q?"

"We're kicking them all out in five. Does your girlfriend know you know all the words to our music?"

He shook his head, knowing damned well I did. "We've never heard of you. Sorry."

Quentin's laugh echoed down the hall and then he led us into a room full of loud, excited people. The girls were half-naked and eyeing the twins like they were a prize, but Quentin ignored them all and whistled at Roman to tell him we had arrived. "Found some strays out back."

"And just like that, all the fun has been sucked out of the room," Roman said bitterly. "Nothing will ruin a good orgy like your older brother showing up."

"I think the phrase you're looking for is 'thank you,'" Harrison said coolly. "I think I just helped you dodge several bullets."

Roman shrugged, standing and tugging on his ripped black jeans. "Whatever. At least you brought your better half, eh?"

Unlike his brother, he pulled me into a bear hug, squeezing tightly, and although they wore different colognes, they still smelled similar. "I am pretty awesome, aren't I?"

"You guys want anything? Drink… food… pussy?" Quentin winked at me when I turned to gawk at him, but his amusement vanished when Harrison smacked the back of his head. "Don't you two have a sound-check to get to?"

Roman smacked Harrison for smacking Q, and the fire in Harrison's eyes scared me until Roman laughed and finally hugged him. "Yeah, we do. Thanks for coming, bro. We always play better with you here."

"Good, just no more smacking. I'm getting jealous," I joked, knowing Harrison would understand exactly what I meant.

It just turned out the twins did, too. They both turned to stare at me with open mouths like they'd never seen a girl admit she liked to be smacked, slapped, or spanked before — and Harrison took their distraction as an opportunity to steal me back.

"This is why this is your first Stagnant Sky show, Briella," he muttered. "Those two become fucking animals when they perform."

"Animals, huh?" I looked them over to tease Harrison, but it only lasted a second before I was caving and melting into his neck. "They still couldn't hold a candle to you."

"That so?" he asked, sliding a broad, strong hand down my back to squeeze my ass as the twins headed out. "We're alone now, kitten. Q promised me we wouldn't be disturbed, so what do you say we find a good spot and we watch the show with my cock buried inside of you?"

I shivered, fingers curling into his suit as I bit my lip. "Is that even possible, Sir?" I asked, practically pleading it to be so.

He looked around quickly, then swept me off my feet and carried me to the side of the stage, setting me down and turning me gently to see. From that spot, we could see most of the stage and the screaming audience beyond, but our bodies were shrouded by darkness. "I'd say so. We'll just have to hope the spotlights don't flip back here… otherwise, ten thousand people will see my pretty, desperate whore stuffed full."

The thought of that being a possibility had my legs clenching together and my knees nearly buckling. "Fuck me, that's hot."

"Oh, I plan on it," he promised, voice rumbling in my ear just as the lights on stage went out completely. I reached back to grab him but found only air, making my heart rate spike and my blood pump harder — but I felt the leather from his undone belt grazing my knee as he sat and pulled me onto his lap.

At first, he wasn't inside me. His nails trailed slowly up my thighs, teasing my dress as Devon's drums set the tone. The faster they got, the higher Harrison's hand traveled, until Mick joined in on bass and those fingers were pulling my panties to the side again.

It was so loud I could moan or scream all I wanted, and in all of our scenes it was technically the most public we'd ever been.

Every single touch was a rush.

He tapped my clit in time to the beat until Roman's voice made the crowd go nuts, then finally lifted me and sank inside of me. I could barely hear him as the vibrations from the amplifiers near us became more intense, but I didn't need to — the way he squeezed my thigh told me I wasn't allowed to come yet.

I rode that high for as long as I could, the lights and fullness had me floating somewhere between heaven and hell, and when I felt him bite my skin, I nearly lost that battle again.

But I wasn't allowed yet.

Wasn't… fucking… allowed.

Those fingers, sinful fingers, found my clit again and pinched, making me scream as my legs jerked and my pussy clenched so hard he smacked it, making me shake. My eyes were so wide staring at the people in the pit, the outline of Quentin's back as he held that guitar, the spotlights that could betray me at any moment that it was almost painful — but Harrison hiked my dress up further until he was palming my exposed breast and forcing my legs further apart.

"Holy fuck!" I yelled, nearly at the top of my lungs, and I wasn't even sure if he could hear me.

He rubbed faster, harder, biting the back of my shoulder until my body was bowing with his cock trapped inside of me and every part of me felt alive — the *thump, thump* of that upbeat punk rock song sending shockwaves through my body until I honestly didn't know if I could obey him this time.

*"Cut my teeth on all the shit you said when you were mad…"*

Not even Roman's angsty lyrics were enough to stop me from reaching back to grip Harrison's hair and out-right begging. "Please, oh fuck, please let me come!"

The double-tap to my thigh gave me permission, and I came just as Roman hit the chorus. *"It's all your fault, we were so good, you tore me down, you said you would, love me till death, but you just lied, take all your shit—"* the drums built — *"and get outta my life!"*

Harrison's fingers didn't stop until I was twitching and gasping, bucking my hips and making him pin us together to stop me from squirming.

*Jesus fuck, I love this man.* My heart-beat felt as if it matched the drums, my ragged breathing masked to the melody of the chorus, and I used all I had to focus on Harrison and clench my cunt. He still hadn't given me what I craved. "Fill me up. Take me… hard."

He stood up still buried inside of me, spinning and putting my knee on the chair he'd just been sitting on. After a moment of not moving at all, he growled low and spun me and that chair around to make me face the crowd, then bent me over and slammed back into me with his hands curled over my shoulders to make me feel every fucking inch.

I'd been mistaken, *this* was the place I never wanted to leave. I loved when he lost control, loved when he used me like I was nothing more than his sex doll, and the pain he caused was absolutely delicious.

The sound of him spanking me was louder to my ears than the music, but he made damned sure I didn't forget where we were when he tugged my head back by my hair and made me watch. Over and over, he slammed into me until I was coming again, then finally gave me what I was after — he wrapped a hand around my throat and squeezed as he filled me up, fucking roughly, erratically until he was pulling out to rub his wet cock all over my ass.

I was a mess, a beautiful fucking mess but I was his, and I couldn't stop the sated laugh that bubbled out of my lips.

Harrison carefully helped me up and spun me to face him, kissing me deeply, madly, like he had since that day in the elevator. I didn't need to hear his words just then — that kiss said everything.

I was his good girl, and no matter what was going on or where we were, Harrison would give me everything I needed.

Just like I would for him.

# The
## Engagement Date

Truth be told, I didn't need a birthday party. I was thankful Harrison cared enough to throw me one, thankful all these people cared enough to show up, but I didn't need one. My thirtieth birthday had passed, and until I hit forty, I didn't see a reason for a huge thing. Weren't those for milestone birthdays? Those, "Hey, I made it another decade," birthdays? Still, I wasn't one to complain.

Especially when we arrived and everyone was wearing masquerade masks.

Harrison knew I'd always wanted to attend one of these parties, and he was giving that to me. Just like he'd given all of my other dreams to me. He liked doing that, making me feel like I was the most special woman in the world, and then later that night treating me like I was a street whore as he bred me.

I liked to think of it as balance.

And all of us could use some balance in our lives, right?

Identifying everyone in masks was ridiculously hard though, and if it weren't for the twins' tattoos, they would have looked like every other tall guy in a suit — at least until I saw the women on their arms. Of course, their plus-ones would look like this… or in Roman's case, plus *two*. Quentin was with his bitchy girlfriend Jess, and based on the look in her eyes and the energy radiating off of her, she had every intention on ruining his night, but it was Roman who made me chuckle. He had a woman on each arm like he was unable to choose who he wanted to bring, but the genuine smiles on their faces stopped me from yelling at him for it.

This wasn't the time or place for that.

I greeted them first anyway because I could at the very least tell who they were, then moved around the gathering pretending I wasn't stressed and like I knew who was hugging me.

I was seconds away from calling Harrison and freaking out on him for disappearing on me when he appeared looking breathless. "Oh, there you are. I need a drink. Where were you?"

"Just attending to some last-minute details," he said flippantly. "Nothing to worry about. Are you having a good time?"

"Yes, better now that you're here." I pulled him in for a kiss and then straightened his mask. "What kind of details? Is there cheesecake hidden somewhere?"

"Several." He nodded, kissing the tip of my nose. "Is my father here yet?"

Grayson Stag was something of an enigma to me — single father of four, eternally single, hard-headed, and so absent from his sons' lives that I'd only seen him once. I wasn't sure I'd have recognized him there even without a mask, but with one?

"No clue." I glanced around like maybe that would help him materialize out of thin air. "My parents are here, but I still haven't found them. Are you sure your dad is coming?"

Harrison shook his head with a tight smile. "No. I never am, but Ethan seems to think he convinced him to come. I'd almost rather he didn't… fucking intimidating."

The thought of Harrison being intimidated by anyone had a shiver traveling up my spine, making me naturally gravitate even closer to him. "Where is Ethan? I haven't seen him yet, did he come alone?"

"No. He's helping me with those last-minute details, so I should probably go check on him. Where are your parents, though? I should say hello."

I narrowed my eyes at him and pulled out my phone. "If this whole place sings to me, I'm leaving," I deadpanned, half-joking, half-serious.

It didn't take long to find my parents once my mom said they were near the snacks, and after some swift hugs, I grabbed a cookie for myself and took a breath. "You eating enough snacks, Dad?"

His eyes widened as he stopped mid-refill, glancing down guiltily at the plate full of little cakes and brownies. "There's no such thing, Bear. Have I taught you nothing?"

"I'm afraid neither of us have," Harrison said, gently taking my elbow to tell me silently that he wanted to leave. "It was great to see you both."

It was abrupt and weird, but both of my parents winked at him. Fucking winked. So I rounded on the weakest link, the one with the mouthful of sugar. "What's going on?" I snatched a brownie bite off his plate. "I don't like when people sing the happy birthday song, you all know this."

"Mmhm," my dad hummed. "Know that, Bear. No singing. Harrison?"

He turned pleading eyes to my boyfriend, who looked equally trapped. "Um…"

"I would rather be trapped in an elevator for *twelve* fucking hours than hear this crowd of thirty-something people sing to me off-tune. Got it?" I pointed my snack at him knowing damn well I'd get spanked for it later, but it was my birthday. I could be bratty if I wanted to.

Sure enough, his eyes flashed. "Bold of you, Briella," he growled, snatching that brownie and popping it into his mouth. "You have three minutes before the music starts, so eat now. I'll be back."

He disappeared into the crowd like fucking Houdini, leaving me with two parents who were actively trying to act like they couldn't see me.

## 11 DATES

*I hate you all,* I thought to myself, then spotted Ethan through the crowd all by himself. "Bingo. I'll be back," I rushed away and cornered the sex therapist where he stood, narrowing my eyes up at him with my arms crossed. "You forgot to put your mask back on. What's going on, Eth? I feel like therapists feel strongly against lying."

His dark eyes matched Harrison's along with his short, black hair, but unlike Harrison, Ethan kept his scruff to a minimum.

"I plead the fifth. I'm sure, as a paralegal, you understand the importance of my rights," he quipped. "You may be terrifying, Bri… but I'm more scared of Harrison."

I groaned, flipping to a new tactic as soon as I got my composure. "How are you? Are you here with anyone?"

"Fine, and yes. She's… busy," he deflected. "Are you here with anyone?"

"Newly single," I quipped. "My boyfriend decided he hated me."

The color drained from Ethan's face. "In the last five minutes? What the fuck?"

"Oh god, you're an idiot. Bye," I laughed as I walked away, shaking my head at the hopeless Stag men and made my way back toward the snack bar — but before I could make it, the music started.

Finding a dancing partner was easy seeing as my favorite co-worker Tessa was there. Having her back after her maternity leave the last couple months was already night and day to that long year without her. "Glad to be out without a kid on your arm?" I asked, taking her hand as she led me deeper onto the dance floor.

"It feels weird. I want to say yes, but I keep checking my phone to see if the sitter called. I kinda hate it," she admitted, fixing her mask. "But I also needed this, so thank you for inviting me!"

"Of course. And no pressure to stay late, I'm sure I'll ditch this party earlier than most." Harrison had already edged me that morning and there was no way he wouldn't give me a mind-blowing orgasm on my birthday.

*Speaking of Harrison… where the fuck is he?*

I glanced around to find him but couldn't identify anyone around us, and as the dance floor got more crowded, I was bumped into and shoved until I lost Tessa, too.

Frustrated, I attempted to move back to the sidelines only to be stopped by people blocking my way. By this point, I was sure there was more than the thirty people I'd thought we'd invited, because making it out of that crowd was becoming increasingly impossible. For a moment, it felt like herding cattle — I just couldn't tell if I was the herder… or the fucking cattle. "Harrison!" I growled, spinning around to try and find an exit on the other side.

I was trapped. My head swam, making me close my eyes tightly to ground myself — I wasn't really trapped, I wasn't on an elevator. I was at a party. I was *fine*.

When I opened my eyes again though, my jaw dropped. All the people who had just been boxing me in were now several feet away, standing in a circle around me — all facing me with their masks on — and the music slowed down.

*Oh, fuck me. Where is he?* My heart hammered in my chest as I looked around at all of them, wishing my mask blocked my heated cheeks as some of them finally parted.

Harrison walked forward, smiling almost sheepishly as he approached me in that gaping, empty space. "Dance with me, my beautiful Briella."

"Seriously?" I whispered, taking his hand without hesitation and releasing a breath as he pulled me in. "You've been hiding from me tonight."

He shook his head softly, wrapping me up in his arms and swaying slowly. "Not hiding, kitten. Prepping."

33

"Prepping what? My asshole hasn't been touched all day." I smiled, just happy to be in his arms again.

"Not that. Just dance with me, beautiful. You're okay." His lips brushed the top of my head, and I caught a fleeting glimpse of the guests still standing in that damned circle before I laid my head against his chest and let myself breathe, forgetting all about them.

Harrison kept me steady, moving gently, until the music changed again. He looked almost nervous as he took my hand and spun me around, and when I faced him again, I knew why.

He was down on one knee with a tiny black box in his hand, staring up at me like I was precious.

"Briella May Lewis… marry me."

"Oh fuck!" I stopped breathing entirely, eyes locked on the gorgeous, dominant man on his knee for me. I couldn't think — I was almost positive my heart stopped beating, and when I attempted to speak, all that came out was a choked-out, whispered, "I hate you."

I didn't mean it, not in the slightest, I was apparently just destined to ruin everything nice in my life.

"Is that a yes?" he asked, but the mask he was wearing couldn't hide the sudden nerves in his eyes.

"Of course it is." I climbed into his lap, not giving a shit who was watching us anymore. Tears fell from my eyes as I pulled off our masks and kissed him, my hands shaking as I gripped his face. "Yes. Yes. A thousand times, yes. I love you."

"I love you more." He kissed me deeper, then pulled back to slip the ring on my finger as our spectators cheered. "Happy birthday, my beautiful girl. I know you didn't want a party, but I'd hoped we'd still have something worth celebrating. And now we do… you're mine."

"Yours, always." I let him wipe away my happy tears and stared into the only eyes I ever cared to stare into again. "You sure you want to be trapped with me again, Sir?"

I bit my lip and reached between us to grip his cock through his slacks, knowing almost everyone was still watching us, but the change in his gaze was worth it.

"Devil woman," he whispered. "I'll be spanking you for this when we get home, but for now… let go. Your father is watching and barely gave me his blessing as it was."

"Did he?" I grinned. "Wouldn't have made a difference to me. I'm yours."

I complied though, letting him help me to my feet and kiss me again like he'd never get enough. I could hardly hear the cheers or the congratulations that were thrown around the rest of the night, all I cared about was him, and the fact that he was mine.

Harrison fucking Stag was mine.

# The Dinner Date

## Harrison

Work was exhausting. I was beginning to hate being a lawyer — the long hours, the paperwork I was making a conscious effort not to push off, the technicalities, the assholes who worked alongside me — and if it weren't for Briella, I likely would've quit.

But she always made things better.

Coming home to her every night was a blessing that I'd never take for granted, no matter how difficult things got. Whether she was happy or sad, tired in the early evening or wide awake in the middle of the night, she always knew exactly how to take the edge off for me… even if she made me work for it.

This day, however, I wasn't sure even Briella could make me feel better. I was exhausted, irritable, I'd suffered a pretty big setback in the case I was arguing that would lead to even more long hours and agitation — and I'd just gotten word that Roman had been arrested.

Again.

I wasn't going to bail him out for once, so I drove straight home and set my briefcase down after a brief, clipped "hello" to Bri.

"Hi," she responded, a nervousness radiating off of her. "You okay, handsome?"

She reached out and pulled me in, and just like that, I felt stupid for ever doubting her. "I'm okay." I kissed her head, breathing in the scent of her hair as her slender arms wrapped around me. "Just a typical day between work and Roman. How are you?"

"I'm good. Are you hungry? Dinner's in the oven."

"My beautiful good girl. You spoil me, you know that?" I whispered, kissing all down the side of her face until I got to her lips. "Thank you for not being a brat today."

"I know what my man needs. No brat tonight, just your good girl and some dinner." She kissed my lips again and pulled away, taking my hand to lead me toward the kitchen.

The oven was off when we got there, making me wonder how the hell long I'd been at work — but a cold dinner was better than no dinner, so I grabbed the oven mitts just in case and opened the door... then froze.

On the middle shelf, on a single cookie sheet, sat a single hamburger bun.

Nothing else.

Just a plain hamburger bun.

I sighed, pulling off the mitts and dropping them on the counter with a thud. "Briella."

"Yes, Sir?" When I looked at her this time those nerves had returned, her fingers dancing anxiously along her stomach as she stared at me like she was waiting for something.

"Is there a hamburger hidden in the microwave? Ham, maybe? Am I on a scavenger hunt for dinner?" I asked, half annoyed, half amused.

"No," she chewed her lip. "What's in the oven?"

I glanced back at it like I'd missed something. "A hamburger bun."

"A hamburger what?"

My lips parted as I stared at her with confusion and a little bit of concern. "Bun, Briella. A bun. There's a bun in the ov—"

*A bun in the oven.*

The once-steady beating of my heart was now erratic, stuttering, rapid as my eyes dropped to the way her fingers were gently splayed over her stomach.

"You…?"

## JENSEN

"Yes," she whispered, taking one tentative foot forward. "It's why I've been so nauseous and grouchy. You put a baby in me. We're having a baby."

My knees gave out. I couldn't breathe with how elated I was — couldn't speak, I was too lightheaded. I tugged her closer, lifting her shirt and kissing that wonderful, beautiful belly over and over again until I had tears in my eyes and Bri raked her slender fingers through my hair.

"I love you," she sniffled. "I love you so much."

"And I love you both," I whispered, standing slowly and lifting her off her feet. The shift in my mood was so sudden and violent that I laughed unexpectedly, kissing her again as I carried her upstairs. "I'll order dinner."

"Sorry I didn't cook. I was just so excited I had to figure out how to tell you."

I shook my head quickly, kissing her over and over as I laid her gently on the bed. "Don't apologize, Briella.

**41**

You've got my child in you. You'll never have to apologize for anything again."

She grinned at that, letting me see first-hand that she would be holding me to that. "I have something else you can eat, Sir."

Slowly, she spread her legs, inviting me in. The wet spot on her panties was so fucking hot that I didn't bother taking them off — I slid between her thighs and licked up the fabric as I held her gaze, ignoring the awkward taste of cotton and drinking in the scent of her, instead.

She cussed, her head falling back with a happy sigh. "I've been so fucking wet."

Briella Lewis, half-naked, pregnant, and soaking through her fucking panties in my bed…

This is what I'd waited all those years for. I growled low, biting the fabric with my teeth and pushing it to the side so I could taste her for real — one hand splayed over her stomach to remind her she was mine, all mine, and my tongue deep in her juicy, delicious cunt until she writhed and threatened to squish my skull between her thighs.

"Oh, fuck! Sir, I— please!"

I was so hard against that goddamn mattress that I could've poked a hole in it, but with the way she was screaming my name, I fucking snapped.

I tore some of the buttons off my shirt trying to strip, and didn't bother taking my old college tee off Briella's body as I climbed back up and slammed inside her. I bunched up the fabric and held that shirt up by her neck so I could watch her gorgeous tits bounce as I pistoned into her, thinking of nothing but her, our child, and the fact that she was fucking mine.

"Good girl," I grunted. "Knew it would take one day. Filled you up so fucking good—"

"So good, always fill me so good. Can I come? Oh please!" She scratched down my arms with a groan, and I was dying to feel her throb and pulse around me.

"Do it, kitten. Come for me… now."

I let go of her shirt to lift her hips and drove myself into her taut body harder, faster, deeper, until the headboard was leaving dents in the drywall and I'd forgotten to breathe completely.

I'd never let go with her like that. I'd always been careful, riding a line between pleasurable pain and potential injury, but now? I couldn't bring myself to hold back, not when she was moaning and twitching underneath me. She yelled my name as she came, squeezing the life out of my aching cock with tears in her eyes.

"Good girl," I whispered. "My beautiful Briella… fuck." I dropped down to kiss the tears from her cheeks as I rolled my hips impossibly deep, feeling that hot, wet squeeze and falling apart a little above her. "God, I love you."

## JENSEN

For the first time, I came inside of her without thinking about getting her pregnant — I was thinking of how long I'd waited for her to truly be mine, to have a part of me rooted inside of her and growing, changing, bringing life to our lives. Of how beautiful she would be with a swollen belly, rounder cheeks and milk-heavy breasts. How I couldn't wait to spoil her every second of this pregnancy, and all the ones that would follow.

The way I'd live for them, die for them, kill to protect them.

My thoughts raced down a track of flash-forward visions for so long that I barely noticed burying my face in her neck and holding her so close, she was squirming.

"Harrison!" she laughed, making me blink and sit back up again.

"Oh. Hi," I smiled. "I'm sorry, I was already thinking about how gorgeous you're going to be in a few months."

"Are you sure you'll still want me if I'm huge and so uncomfortable I'm bitchy?"

I gently kissed her. "Briella, I've put up with you at your brattiest, and without you carrying our child. I can't wait to watch you both grow." I kissed her again, slowly, pouring all the truth of my words into it — I needed her to understand exactly how serious I was, because the next few months wouldn't be all ice cream at midnight and foot massages.

She was about to learn exactly how possessive, protective, and utterly insane I could really be.

I just hoped she was ready for it.

# The First Birth Date

If I thought Harrison was protective before I got pregnant, I didn't know shit. If he was home, I was hardly allowed out of bed. He doted on me, that was for sure, but him not even wanting me to get the food from the porch after it was delivered was ridiculous. Did he really think our delivery guy would hurt me in some way? Or was he *that* worried that my water would break on the short trip down the stairs like this was some cheesy movie?

Most of the time, I didn't mind, but being nine months pregnant and hungry had my patience wearing a little thin. "I can just grab it. You're in the damn shower."

"No, you cannot," he said firmly, poking the shower curtain. "Just give me a moment, I'm almost done, my love."

"I'm so hungry," I complained, rubbing my belly in a way that always made him weak the second he peeked his head out. "I'll be downstairs."

I rushed out before he could stop me, making it all the way down before it happened. The gush of it made me gasp, the rush of warm liquid making me spread my legs in horror as a small puddle formed on the hardwood floor between my feet. I couldn't believe it was actually happening, especially before I got to eat my fucking food. "Fuck me," I muttered, then called out for the man that was about to murder me for not listening and staying in bed. "Harrison!"

The soaking wet, naked idiot slipped on the bottom stair and barely caught himself. "Briella! Is it — are you—?"

I met his gaze with true fear in my eyes. "He doesn't want to wait for his due date. Fuck, I— my water broke."

"Okay," he said, hands out and eyes wide. "We've prepared for this, so breathe. Get in the car, I'll put some pants on and grab the bag."

"I want a shower," I argued, knowing it would do nothing. "That shit went everywhere, can you get me a towel?"

"I'll bring one out to you. Go get in the car, Briella. If you're still standing here when I come back, I'll carry you."

He bolted back up the stairs, and I stared down at the mess again before waddling over for the paper towels. Contractions hadn't truly kicked in yet, and I knew my water breaking was just the beginning of this long adventure so I had some time. Once the floor was as clean as I could get it while still slowly leaking, I made my way to his gorgeous car and stared at it. I didn't want to sit and get it dirty, so I waited for Harrison and that towel, but before he could come out to the garage my first true contraction hit. It made all of those Braxton Hicks look like child's play. "Oh fuckfuckfuck!"

I gripped my lower belly with a groan and leaned against the door, but Harrison was there in an instant. "I got you, beautiful girl. Okay. In you go."

I let him help me into the car, hastily pressing a towel between my legs as that contraction subsided. "Okay, that was less than a minute, but we still have time. I— I wanted those fucking fries."

He closed my door, then open and closed the back door before climbing in the driver's seat — and the smell of salt hit me a split second before he put the container in front of me. "Did you honestly think I'd forget the fries?"

"God, I love you." I grabbed it, shoveling them into my mouth like I was an animal, but I was beyond caring by this point. There was no way they'd let me eat once we got to the hospital, and with how painful that contraction was, I wasn't sure I'd even want to. "I'm scared," I admitted between bites.

"I know." He squeezed my hand, then brought it to his lips to kiss. "But you're going to be fine, Bri. You and our little Arlo both."

I smiled down at my belly and rubbed it, allowing myself to feel all the emotions I needed to feel. Our baby was coming, a baby made from love and passion, one Harrison had always wanted and I didn't know how much I needed. Arlo would change everything. He'd brighten our lives, even with the sleepless nights and endless diaper changes, and aside from being scared, I was excited to start this next chapter of our lives. I fed my little Arlo some more fries, hissing when he kicked out at my hand and another contraction started. Somehow I got the feeling that was my baby boy letting me know he was ready to enter the world, and if he was anything like his

51

father… he'd be coming on his own time, not mine.

Ready or not, Arlo was going to be born today.

As it turned out, though… I was way more ready than Harrison. My feral fiancé wouldn't let anyone near me except for the nurses and doctors, which nearly got him thrown out on more than one occasion — but no one could deny the protectiveness and sheer devotion in his eyes as he helped me into the gown and knelt next to my bed.

"I'm not dreaming, right?" he whispered.

I huffed, more uncomfortable by the second. "No. Definitely not fucking dreaming, Har. Maybe I should punch you in the face so you'll believe me?"

He blinked, clenching his jaw slightly. "I wouldn't advise it, but I also won't stop you. Which side of my face do you like more?"

## JENSEN

"Ugh!" I groaned, tugging at the stupid monitors they placed on my stomach, but hearing his heartbeat was comforting. I closed my eyes and melted into it, my breathing calming with Harrison's hand in mine. "I like all of your face."

"Are you sure? That didn't sound convincing," he teased, making me smile slightly.

"I'm sure. I bred with it, didn't I?"

"That is not the body part you bred with, but I'll allow it."

I chuckled. "I don't know, I've sat on your face a few times."

My doctor cleared his throat and bit back a grin. "Glad you two are in good spirits. How's your pain?"

He moved closer, making Harrison's grip on my hand tighten. "Right now like a six, but when the contractions hit, like a nine," I said.

"That's good," he encouraged. "I would check how dilated you are, but seeing as your water broke, we like to avoid that. You're more prone to infection, but if you want me to check, I can."

The thought of Harrison having to sit next to me while he stuck his fingers inside my vagina was laughable, but I declined. "I was four at my last appointment, I think I'll pass for now."

"Good call. It's not really necessary, some just like to know. Based on your contractions, I'd say you're further along than a four now, but time will tell. Have you considered pain medication or an epidural?"

"I have, and I'm going to pass, thank you."

"Alrighty. You stay comfortable and let us know if you need anything at all."

He left, and I smiled over at Harrison in spite of the tightening in my stomach. "You breathing, baby?"

"Who?" he grunted, blinking like an idiot. "What?"

I sighed, wishing he could fit on that bed with me to hold me. "I should have ate more fries."

"I'll sneak them in for you," he assured me. "Whatever you need, Bri. Can I help? Do you need me to push?"

I outright laughed at that. "Yes. That would be helpful. Ugh, what if he rips my asshole? You Stag's have big heads."

"I genuinely don't know how to answer that," he admitted. "But I've seen firsthand how much your holes can stretch, Bri… and our heads aren't that big."

"Yeah… but this is different. Going to have to wait weeks to fuck me again, Harrison. You sure you'll last?" I was teasing him, and the distraction helped me through another contraction as he grimaced from the way I squeezed his hand.

"You still have a mouth," he said flippantly, making me snort.

"Such an asshole," I gasped, the pain intensifying more than any of the others. "Fuck, this one won't end!"

"So call me an asshole again," he pleaded. "Focus on me, Briella. My beautiful, good girl. Yell at me."

Tears welled in my eyes as I met his. "I can't when you look so damn cute. It hurts. Har—"

I groaned loud, arching off the bed as that contraction peaked.

"What?" he rushed out. "Is it time? What do I do? Where the fuck is your doctor?"

How hard I squeezed his hand had to have cut off the circulation, but my man didn't pull back in the slightest until it calmed once again. Hours went by just like that, me screaming more with each passing one, and no matter what position I was in or how attentive Harrison was with his back rubs, I couldn't get comfortable. All of it was painful, but when I was truly in transition... I knew it.

Consciousness faded in and out in waves as the pain forced me into an out-of-body experience and everyone around me felt far away. I could hear them rustling around me as they helped me bring my knees up, but Arlo had *my* patience, not Harrison's. "I have to push! Fucking fuck, it hurts! I should have got the fucking epidural!"

"You can do this, Briella," Harrison urged. "Squeeze me tighter, beautiful. You're so strong."

The rest of his birth was an excruciating haze, one that had me questioning my life as a masochist. Normally I loved pain, but this was something else entirely.

I pushed for so long I thought he'd never come into the world, but when he finally did, my entire world shifted. All of my focus went to the screaming little bundle in the doctor's arms, and I reached out for him with a sob in my chest. "Give me him."

The doctor smiled as he laid the slimy human on my chest and continued checking him out, and only then did my baby stop crying. He knew he was safe with his momma.

"My beautiful, perfect Briella and our beautiful, perfect Arlo," Harrison whispered, kissing all over my face and gently rubbing our baby's chubby little arm. "You did it, Bri. My best girl."

I cried, happy and scared tears, but I knew no matter how terrified I was to take home a living baby, my Harrison would be by my side.

By *our* side… because now we were three.

# The Wedding Date

"Shhh, it's okay Arlo." I rocked my six-month-old after a feeding, trying to calm him down in all the fuss while praying to all the gods that he didn't spit up on my wedding dress.

Tessa reached out to help, but I knew my son, and he wouldn't stop crying in someone else's arms — only mine or Harrison's.

"Let us help," my mom encouraged. "Your hair isn't done."

"I know, but he needs me. He'll calm down in a second."

But Arlo wouldn't calm down.

## 11 DATES

My mom ducked out of the room as I paced and rocked my stubborn baby boy, bringing Harrison back with her a moment later.

"I know it's bad luck to see you before the wedding, but I was told you both needed me. Luck can kiss my ass," Harrison whispered, holding out his arms.

"Thank you," I whispered, melting into his arms with Arlo like I had the time to cuddle. "I think he's stressed, too."

"Can't fathom why either of you are stressed," he said quietly. "This is the best day of our lives. Nothing can go wrong today."

I smiled, believing him wholeheartedly as I calmed against his chest with Arlo right behind me. "Not even my hair?"

"Not even your hair."

"I love you." I pulled back and handed Arlo over, knowing that he was safe with his daddy. "You look so handsome."

"No one will be looking at me, kitten." He whistled softly as he patted Arlo's back, bouncing until he finally burped. "There we are. That was a tough one, huh, buddy?"

The love in Harrison's eyes as he flicked them from Arlo to me had mine watering. Watching the man you love hold and love your child had to be one of the most beautiful things in the world. "Can you believe he's six months already? I think he's ready to watch you make an honest woman out of me."

"Oh, I think even Arlo knows that'll never happen," he teased softly. "You're too much of a brat." He leaned in to kiss me slowly, humming against my lips. "You look stunning, kitten. My beautiful Briella."

"Thank you, Sir. Maybe Arlo will go with my mom now and they'll give us a moment?"

I nipped his lip, gasping quietly as he palmed my ass and squeezed. "That would require us to postpone this wedding, which I'm not willing to do. We're getting married, brat. Right now."

I pouted my bottom lip, loving the way his hand felt on my body and in one swift movement, I pulled Arlo from his arms and handed him to my mom, then wrapped my arms around his neck. "You sure? No cold feet?"

"They've never been warmer. And it's too late to change your mind, so don't try," he growled, flicking his tongue over my earlobe and biting gently. "Going to spank you in this dress later on."

"Please," I gasped, ignoring Tessa as she slipped through the room. "I need you to fuck me in it too."

Harrison gripped my chin softly to steady me, flicking that intoxicating gaze from my lips to my eyes. "We're going to ruin this dress. But for now, let's go show it off."

Parting ways was a struggle, but when my mother and two aunts rushed in the room to kick him out, we didn't really have a choice. I was forced to watch him leave and let my family dote on me, putting the finishing touches on the flowers in my hair and the makeup adorning my face under my glasses, but none of it calmed me down. My hands were still shaking with nerves as I took my place on my father's arm.

"It's okay, Bri," he assured me. "No need to be nervous."

"What if I fall?"

My father kissed my cheek. "Then Harrison would fall with you. I've seen the way he looks at you."

My chest fluttered, his words helping more than I could have ever explained, and as we walked out to the aisle, I felt myself calm. My dad was right, Harrison would never let me fall in any capacity, and I was lucky enough to marry him.

I'd chosen an outdoor wedding, one with tall trees all around us and white lights draped between them so beautifully it looked like we were inside of a waterfall. But regardless of how breathtakingly beautiful it was, all I saw was him.

His tuxedo was jet black and so well-fitted to his muscular body that he didn't quite look real — nor did the expression of wonder, adoration and sheer joy on his face as he watched me slowly step closer to him.

Once the archaic-yet-traditional hand off was made, I squeezed his hands in mine and let myself get lost in his gorgeous green eyes. I'd never wanted anything more than this, than to be his wife.

Everything else melted away. I barely heard the words our officiant said, or the quiet, gorgeous tune Roman was playing. I barely heard Arlo giggling behind me, my aunts tearing up, the sound of Ethan repeatedly smacking Harrison's shoulder in beloved disbelief.

My heart was beating too hard, too fast to really hear any of it… until Harrison's vows.

## JENSEN

"Briella, I make it a point to keep the things you love about yourself at the forefront of your mind. But now… this is about the things that I love the very most about you — your passion, your determination, the grumpy look on your face before you have coffee in the morning, the obsession you have with French fries… and your heart. I could go on to talk about how cute you look when you fog up your glasses or what a hard worker you are, how patient and kind and what a stunningly beautiful, amazing mother you are… but truthfully, we'd be here all day. There isn't anything about you I don't love, Briella May… except your last name. It should've been mine a long time ago, and once it is, I promise you that I will spend every moment of the rest of my life filling every desire, dream and… fantasy you've ever had. I've waited a very, very long time for this day, Briella. I love you."

I smiled, tears filling my eyes at his words. There was no way I could ever top his vows, but something told me that didn't matter. He didn't say pretty lies just to save face, he showed me all of that every single day. "I know, I love you too. Since that night in the elevator I learned to love myself, and I know that's because of you. You helped me learn to live with fear and not shut down with it, something that has helped me every single day and I will forever be thankful. But that's what you do, you build me up so high that I never think low of myself, and I hope with all of me I help you with that too. You're the burger to my fries, the pain to my pleasure, and even when you're a dickbag, I want you right by my side. You're all I need, Harrison. You are my desire, dream and fantasy. Now give me your last name, Mr. Stag. I've waited long enough."

He didn't pause for the ceremonial "I do's," he kissed me right there, lifting me off of my feet and spinning me around — breaking it only to glare at our poor officiant. "Is it done? Is she mine?"

"I— y— I take it you both… do?"

We both said the words at the same time, kissing once again as he presented us to the crowd that was quickly fading away. "I love you," I whispered over and over between kisses, noting how the cheers of our family were actually fading as he carried me away. "Where are we going?"

"Tessa!" he yelled. "Keep our son close. Send everyone else to the reception… I need twenty minutes with my wife."

The word sent wild shivers down my spine as he carried me back to the room I'd gotten dressed in and knelt before me, disappearing under the folds of my dress to tear my panties off. "Oh, fuck! You want to taste your wife, Sir? Feel how wet I am just knowing I'm yours?"

"Yes. Come for me."

He pushed one of my legs over his shoulder and cupped my ass to steady me as he licked and sucked my pussy like he was half-starved and completely insane, and maybe we both were. I didn't hold back, I could care less if anyone walked by and heard my moans. I was his wife, and he was making me feel so damn good I wanted to bask in that feeling forever.

"Fu-ck! I can- can't find your head." I clawed around my dress for it, and when I found my prize, I gripped his hair and rolled against his tongue.

With as desperate and skilled as he was, the first orgasm hit me quickly. I barely had time to tense up before he was standing to push the taste of myself onto my tongue and backing me toward the dresser — but the look in my eyes as he spun me around to face the mirror above it had me staying right where I was at on that blissful edge.

"Make me feel so good, Harrison. Fuck me hard… make me feel it the rest of the night."

"Oh, my beautiful, adorable Briella. I plan on making you feel it for the rest of your *life.*"

His hand slapped my bare ass so hard it echoed and drowned out the sound of him sliding his rock-hard cock inside my soaked cunt, but how quickly my thighs started shaking should have been embarrassing. "Fuck yes… harder. Slap me harder, please."

"Briella," he grunted, fisting the skirt of my dress tighter and spanking me harder. "Tell me I can put another baby in you now. Miss your body like that… how eager, desperate and wet you get, how gorgeous your curves are, your chest and this—" he spanked again— "this ass. Tell me I can."

The way Arlo behaved just an hour ago had me almost saying no, but there was no world where I would deny him. I missed it too, missed how feral and possessive my man was when I had his child inside of me, and even during those sleepless nights I knew I wanted more kids. I wasn't sure we'd ever stop.

"Yes," I gasped. "Put another baby inside me, breed me. I—"

I came again, clenching and choking on whatever the hell I was about to say as he hammered into me, ramming me into that dresser over and over until he was filling me up and fucking it deeper.

"Mine, Briella."

"Yours! All yours… forever." I kissed him, forgetting about everything but my husband for just a few more moments.

Everything else could wait.

# The Second Birth Date

## Harrison

In all my life, in all the thousand lives I'd lived in dreams and fantasies, I'd never — *never* — seen anything or imagined anything quite as beautiful as pregnant Briella.

It dumbfounded me, honestly, struck me dumb, stole all semblance of coherent speech from my mind and ripped the breath from my lungs… and all she was doing was sitting there.

Legs spread with baggy, stained sweats, a baggier t-shirt, her swollen hand splayed over her swollen belly, and glaring at me like she hated me.

My beautiful, perfect Briella.

"What?" I asked, toeing the line between sincerity and playfulness. "It almost looks like you want to hit me."

"Maybe I do." It was a rare moment of quiet as Arlo napped upstairs. "Maybe it's our one-year anniversary and I want to slap you in a very non-kinky way for doing this to me again."

She waved at her giant belly, a playfulness in her eyes as well as a truth I wasn't sure I wanted to test. "Briella… it's a little late to be having second thoughts about our first daughter," I reminded her gently. "If you'd like to smack me, go for it. Just don't blame me when I get a boner whether you mean it in a kinky way or not."

She laughed, spreading her legs slightly in a way that felt inviting. "I like when you get a boner, Harrison."

"Good. Then strip for me, kitten. You may not feel up to a fancy date to celebrate our anniversary, but I bet you're up for multiple orgasms, hm?" I slipped slowly, deliberately down to my knees, chuckling quietly at the ketchup stains on her sweats. "And maybe laundry, but I'll handle that, too."

She huffed, struggling slightly with undressing but it was nothing I couldn't help her with. "You always keep me ready for multiple orgasms, Sir. Just seeing you on your knees…" She sighed, adorably irritated that I always knew my way around her moods.

"If you'd prefer I didn't…"

"No, no… stay. Please. Even like this you make me feel beautiful."

I frowned up at her. "Even? Especially like this. I'd keep you like this forever if I could."

She chuckled. "I don't doubt it, but I think you like the breeding act too much to keep me like this. Don't you love coming inside this soaked cunt and breeding me? That feeling when you find out another one took and you impregnated me?"

"Yes," I admitted. "It's the whole process, Briella. Not just one part. I love breeding you, knowing that I'm making you mine over and over, knowing that for roughly nine months… you literally have a piece of me inside of you at all times. But look at you now." I traced my fingers over the stretch marks on her stomach, her ass. "Goddess marks… and let's not pretend I haven't thought about milking you a time or two."

"Fucking fuck!" she gasped, twitching under my touch. "Why is that so hot?"

I hummed happily, pushing her legs apart further. "Because you were made for me, Briella. You're mine, and so is this body. Now come for me."

Now, I was also wholeheartedly positive she'd never taste better than she did when she was pregnant. I wasn't naive — I knew at least part of it was sweat, no matter what she did to clean up — but the way her flavors danced on my tongue had me feeling fucking insatiable.

She moaned, the thud of her head falling back against her chair reaching my ears. I felt her hands move to play with her swollen breasts, and I... let my mind wander.

To what it would feel like to bite and suck her sensitive nipples, to be the cause of the little sigh of relief she lets out when some of the pressure lessens.

To drink from her like it would give me life, too.

I must've gotten carried away, because I almost missed how hard she was coming when her thighs clenched around my head and attempted to pop it. "Harrison! Fuck me!"

No way I could've said no to her, but I held back as I slid inside her. I couldn't degrade her like this, couldn't slap her or be rough with her like I wanted to. She was so, so strong... but uncomfortable enough without me literally fucking her like an animal in heat.

"So wet for me, Briella. Always such a good girl for me."

"Thank you," she moaned. "You always make me so wet; fucking love your mouth!"

"And I love—" and there, it was impossible not to notice the liquid running through her fingers and down her hands as she squeezed her chest, impossible not to need a taste — "all of you, kitten. All."

*Fuck it. She may never let me knock her up again.*

I leaned in, brushing her hand away with my nose and sucking her nipple into my mouth before either of us could get freaked out. "Oh, g— Harrison! Sir!" I felt her body begin to tremble as she clenched around me, and fucking hell, I couldn't describe what it tasted like.

I wasn't sure it *had* a taste — at least not one that overpowered the aftertaste of pussy on my tongue — but the way it felt to have it squirting into my mouth, to feel her pussy throbbing and getting wetter by the second, contracting around me until I was lost in her, it, her milk filling my mouth and making my cock fucking ache with the need to fill her up again.

I felt the rush of warm come gush around my cock, her beautiful gasp filling my ears as she clawed along my skin. "Feels fucking — Harrison!"

So much for not fucking her like a literal animal. I switched sides, spreading my knees a little further on the carpet and bracing her better against the front of the couch in my lap, ignoring the way my back was cramping from the way I had to bend around her belly.

So fucking worth it, so fucking beautiful.

So fucking… wet.

Unusually wet… and not that I was complaining, but she pulled my hair with a grip and force reminiscent of the way she tried to break my hand

when she'd given birth to Arlo —
when she'd been in labor with Arlo.

"Bri-e- oh, fuck." I came so hard I
almost blacked out, but the sound of
her growl kept me conscious enough
to realize she was in actual pain. The
problem was my Bri loved pain, and it
was evident by the way her nipples
were still leaking and her body was still
twitching. "Okay," I breathed, pulling
out and carefully helping her sit on the
ground. "Are you in labor, Briella? Do
we need to go?"

"No, I just… squirted?" She tried
and failed to sit up, groaning as more
liquid gushing out. "Why's it still happening? I'm not in labor. Not yet.
We're busy."

I blinked down at the growing mess
on our floor. "Um…"

"Fuck!" she growled, collapsing in
defeat. "Your kids have minds of their
own."

"Just like their headstrong, incredible mother," I praised, standing carefully to help her up. "But don't lie.

You're at least a little excited that the playing field is about to be leveled out. Two guys, two girls."

Bri grinned. "I am. I'm sure she'll love all of Arlo's toys, but he seems to gravitate toward babies and animals more than anything. I love that we don't gender their toys."

She took a deep breath, giving me a look that confirmed my suspicions. Whether she wanted to admit it or not, Blaire Stag was ready to make her debut — and our wedding anniversary was about to be a birthday, too.

One day, Bri would probably strangle me for the timing here… but I'd find a thousand little ways to make it up to her.

Always.

# The Cut-Off Date

"Blaire! Stop messing with your brother. He doesn't want to wrestle." My toddler stomped her foot in a way that would have gotten me spanked as a child, but luckily for her, I was trying hard not to carry on my parents' bad habits. "Don't get an attitude, girl. Arlo doesn't like playing like that, he never has."

"He *never* wants to play what I want to play!" she argued, making our second daughter wake up in my arms. Having three children under five was *not* how I imagined my life would go, but I wouldn't change it for the world… even when I wanted to rip out my hair. Piper screamed, making my nipples burn with an unwanted let-down, and as I attempted to get her latched on, Blaire tugged Arlo's hair and made him cry out. "Blaire!"

Arlo shoved her off of him and ran over to me, trying to climb into my lap with his seven-week-old sister. "Blaire is mean. I don't want Piper to be mean, too."

I didn't know what to say to that, but when all three of them started crying, I was five seconds away from joining them. Luckily for me, my savior entered the house just in time, rushing over to scoop Blaire up like she was the victim. "Harrison, she's just mad because *Arlo* is mad at the fact that she pulled his hair. Don't let her play you."

"Noted, but I'm also very likely going to ignore you. This sassy little spitfire is so much like you that I'm afraid she'll never do anything wrong," he said fondly, but then wagged his finger in Blaire's face with a stern expression that had her pouting and hiding her face in his neck. "Arlo, come with me, too. I'll fix you both a snack while your mom feeds your sister... unless you two have suddenly decided you don't like snacks anymore?"

"No!" Blaire yelped, straightening up with a horrified expression. "I love snacks."

"Of course you love snacks, I made you. Go on, Arlo. Go with daddy for a snack."

He clung to me for a moment longer before he walked over to take Harrison's hand, and I smiled fondly at my strong, sensitive boy. No amount of books could have prepared me for Arlo's needy, loving personality, but I loved him exactly the way he was.

Once I had a moment to breathe, I realized how perfect our little family was. Sure, we didn't always get along, but all families were like that, and as long as I continued to raise them close... I believed that bond would last a lifetime.

Or at least I hoped.

A little while later I went to join them with a sleeping, milk-drunk baby in my arms, finding them in a scene I wanted a picture of. Harrison was sitting on the floor with his back against the counter and one kid sleeping on each thigh, his expression soft, but almost as exhausted as mine. "Did Piper get her fill?" he asked softly. "I think they're all ready for bed."

"I think so too," I agreed, moving closer slowly to keep them from waking. "She got her fill, but I hope you did too. My baby-maker is closed."

The little bit of joy that had been on his face vanished. "Closed for the night?"

It was almost enough to have me backtracking. I hated seeing disappointment on his gorgeous face. "No, Sir. No more babies, but we can practice all you want still."

"Briella," he pleaded as quietly as he could, standing to carry a kid in each arm. "Put Piper down. I'll get these two settled, then get on your knees for me in our room."

I nodded, knowing that conversation was far from over as we parted ways and got our adorable little humans into bed. Piper took her pacifier like a champ and let me go quicker than I anticipated, but it worked out in my favor. I was already on my knees by the time Harrison entered. "Sir."

I bowed my head, nervous about the energy he was putting off as he gripped my chin and forced my gaze up. "How long have you been thinking about this?"

"Since Piper ripped open the scar Arlo's head caused. Since our two oldest decided they wanted a Stag Civil War in our home. It isn't something that I feel continuously, Harrison. It hits me when I'm overwhelmed or exhausted. You don't think about it?"

"No," he said honestly. "Not beyond how many people my salary can realistically support. I always wanted a lot of kids, Briella… but it's your body.

Ultimately, it's your decision, and I told you way back when we first started dating that I would never force this on you. So, if three is your limit… then fine," he said, but not even the Great Harrison Stag could disguise the devastation in his eyes.

He wasn't done yet, no matter what he said.

Still, I nodded and decided to call his bluff. "Thank you. Our family is perfect just the way it is."

He jerked slightly like he wasn't expecting me to double down, then released my chin with a sigh. "Okay. We're both exhausted and you're delusional, so let's sleep. We'll revisit this in the morning."

I grinned to myself as I stood and let him put me to bed. The fact that he called me delusional was hilarious, as was the fact that he let me sleep so long my boobs were full and leaking on my shirt. When I went to get Piper for some release, I found Harrison asleep with three kids around him, the baby with a bottle in her lap and the other two sprawled out like it was their job, and my sweet, sweet man exhausted between them. I snuck off to get my phone for a picture, stole Piper from him so she could drink some more milk from the source, then laid her back in the crib so I could make breakfast.

By the time they all joined me, I had the tables set and their juices poured… it was amazing what a full night's sleep could do for a person. "Morning, my beautiful family. Everyone sleep well?"

"Of course," Harrison lied, pulling me in to kiss my temple. "I realized about an hour or so after you fell asleep that my time with adorable toddlers was ticking, since my beautiful, strong wife brutally cut me off. I'll be sleeping with the three of them until further notice."

"I don't agree to that," I argued, wrapping my arms around his waist to pin him there as the older two argued

JENSEN

over the syrup. "I need you to hold me too."

"Fine, then they'll be sleeping with us," he said flippantly. "I'm sure that'll cut into our playtime, but that's not a big deal. We'll have decades once these three are grown."

He was never going to stop with the side comments, so the only way to get him to admit he wasn't okay with it was to go along with him. "You're right. Decades of playtime."

"Mhm." He kissed my forehead twice, holding there for a moment. "Or we could compromise."

"Do you have some sort of issue with the new-but-current arrangement, Mr. Stag?"

"Yes," he growled, glancing over my shoulder and then meeting my eyes. "It's not fair. I didn't get to give your pregnant body a proper goodbye."

I laughed, I couldn't help it. "A proper goodbye? And what would a proper goodbye look like?"

"Probably a lot of me crying, licking your pussy until you pass out, and me kissing every curve of your body while I worship your stretch marks. A lot of midnights where I wake you up with my cock because I can't resist you."

All of that sounded tempting. "Maybe you should go down on me and then ask how I feel again."

"I'm also prepared to throw in a caveat that if you give me one more, you can use my body however you see fit each day that you're pregnant. Dishes, sex, piggyback rides, make me eat foods I hate, I don't care. Just give me another son… and yes. We'll continue this after my second breakfast."

The seriousness in his voice had me biting my lip and wanting to rush through first breakfast, and when the time finally came, it was more like brunch. The kids went down for their naps and Harrison was on me, carrying me to our bed and tossing me on it without a word.

# JENSEN

"I have to say… that was a good fucking argument this morning, baby."

"Did you expect anything different?" he quipped, ripping my shorts from my body and slapping my pussy through my panties. "I had precedence prepared, too. I never come to an argument unprepared."

He slapped the inside of my thigh, making me twitch and see just how serious he was. "I know you don't. Let's hear it, big guy."

I bit my lip, gasping quietly as he pinched my thigh and slid my panties off. "On December 5, three years ago, you promised me four children. You said you thought my parents did it right with my brothers and I." I His thumb pressed my clit and tapped just enough to drive me nuts, a steady, pulsing beat of pleasure. "We also agreed to buy a house with seven bedrooms."

*Jesus fuck, this man is good.* "Did I?" I gasped, squirming slightly as I let him have his way with me. "We could make it a guest room."

"Briella," he growled, lowering down to bite my pussy and shove two fingers inside of me.

"Fuck!" I yelled, reaching down to grip and tug on his hair. "You want one more, baby? Need to breed my body one more time?"

The rumble in his chest went straight through his tongue to my clit. "Yes, Briella. One more time. Please?"

"Oh, g— you're so hot when you say please. More," I pushed, seconds away from caving because in truth he wasn't the only one who wanted a big family.

He didn't disappoint me.

That tongue took me apart as he buried his face in my cunt, licking and sucking and biting and pulling back long enough to slap until I was gushing for him and giving him something else to taste, but I made him work for that orgasm.

Holding back was a struggle, one that had me holding my breath and tugging on the sheets hard, but that man never let up. He ripped two more orgasms from me in a matter of minutes and when he finally came up for air I knew I couldn't deny him. "Okay, Sir. One more…"

I had no idea when he'd pulled his cock out during that, but there was nothing standing in his way as he pushed my legs to my chest and eased into me. "Say it, Briella."

I moaned, still addicted to the way he felt when he entered my body, to how it felt when we became one. "I want you to put your baby inside me. I want to create one more beautiful human with you."

"Yeah?" he grunted, bottoming out and rolling his hips. "You like it when I come inside you, kitten? Breed you? Come so deep it ends up in your fucking lungs?"

"Fuck yes! I love feeling you lose control as you take me and mark my insides as yours. Love when you claim all of me. Harder… fuck me deeper, baby. Aim for the fucking wall so you get your son."

My husband bent my body in half, fucking me into that mattress until his moans sounded angry and I was squirting around his cock in bursts — I would never get used to it. No matter how many years we spent together, it was impossible to get used to how good this man made me feel. "Come on, baby. Breed me."

"One more time," he breathed, fire in his eyes and a passion in each thrust that told me he was absolutely aiming for the wall. "Fuck… take it," he grunted, pinning my hips down and tipping over, grinding deep. "Take it, kitten. All of it. You're mine… always."

I groaned as I felt him throb inside me, loving the palpable possession all around us as he claimed me once again. Whether it took or not, we didn't know, but that wasn't the point.

## JENSEN

A fourth baby was happening, and aside from the natural nerves of creating more life, I was glad for it.

I wasn't quite done carrying his children, either.

## The
## Twin Date

My last pregnancy had to have been the hardest. I had more morning sickness than ever, walking around was a fucking chore, and to make everything worse… I was twice as large by the time we found out we were pregnant again.

I didn't even have the energy to go to our ultrasound appointment, but Harrison was far too excited for me to ruin it, so I forced a smile and let him dote on me the entire morning.

Ethan and his wife stopped by to watch the three older kids for us, and although it took me forever to get out of the car, I found myself getting more excited as we made our way into the waiting room. "You ready to see if you aimed for the wall?"

"Pretty sure I broke down the wall and aimed past it," he muttered, eyes dancing with anticipation. "But yes. No matter what, I'm going to be happy. You're incredible, Briella. My beautiful Bri…"

It looked like he wanted to eat me out right there, so I bit my lip for the briefest of seconds and then tugged him along to take a seat. "So if it's another girl, are you going to try and convince me to have one more?"

"Yes, but that's not important right now," he lied. "As long as they're healthy, I'm good."

I chuckled, my stomach fluttering when they called us back, and I could tell he knew how nervous I was by how hard I was squeezing his hand.

"It's going to be fine, Briella. I promise." Harrison kissed my knuckles before helping me up onto the bed, and I fought the urge to kill him for putting me in this position again as the nice woman in front of me took all my vitals and asked me a million questions.

In pregnancies past, changing into the gown was always something fun and a little dirty — Harrison would stay to help and end up bending me over to tease me for a while, but it wasn't possible this time. I'd thrown on a dress for once, so our ultrasound tech had easy access to me, and I had easy access to throat chop Harrison when that grainy, black and white picture revealed one of my worst fucking nightmares.

"Your machine is broken. We need another one," I said matter-of-factly, not taking another look at the screen.

"It's not broken," my asshole husband said quickly. "Briella… they're…"

"Boys," the tech finished. "Both boys, blood test confirmed."

Boys. Both. Twins. There was no fucking way I had two Stag boys inside my body when I'd barely agreed to one more. "There… no, I… we wanted a fourth child."

"And it seems your fourth wanted another brother," she said.

"Told you I broke the wall down."

Harrison beamed, and I had to shake my head to ensure I wasn't dreaming. I wasn't. "Fuck that wall. Twins? Twins, Harrison!"

"I feel like this is your body's way of punishing you for trying to tell me no," he joked, quiet and growly, making our tech excuse herself for a few moments to give us some privacy. "Brat."

If he thought I was a brat with my other pregnancies, he hadn't seen anything yet. "You know this means I get double the spoiling, right? Double the fries and back rubs?" He nodded, kissing me hard — all possession and promise and heat, and I reached down to palm him. "Enjoy it, baby. Make sure you say your proper goodbyes to my pregnant body like you wanted. I'm going to be even bigger this time."

# 11 DATES

"Bri." He pulled back with tears in his eyes as he feverishly began kissing down my chest to my belly, hands shaking as they slid down my body. "Twins, Briella. You're incredible… fucking incredible."

Seeing him this way had me soft in seconds. "Twins, Sir. I'd blame you if that was how it worked. I had no clue twins were in my family, but I like seeing you this happy."

"Bed rest, Bri. Until those boys are born — maybe even after. You won't lift a finger for yourself, and if you think I was spoiling you before…" Harrison trailed off as we were joined again, and the tech smiled sheepishly at us both.

"Everything okay?" she asked.

"More than okay. He was just promising me a lifetime of well-deserved spoiling," I smiled like the true brat I was at him, but not even that could wipe the sheer adoration from his eyes.

"I was. Can we see them again? The twins?"

"One more time. I know how shocking that first time was, so I'll make an exception." She winked and turned the machine back on, and this time, I truly let it sink in.

We were having twins.

"Shit," I whispered, eyes watering as my emotions bubbled over. "Harrison."

"I'm here, Briella," he said softly, threading his fingers through mine and kissing my hand. "I love you, my beautiful Bri."

"I love you too. I love our babies… all five of them."

~

Harrison hadn't been joking. I'd hardly left the bed this pregnancy when he was around, but when he wasn't, I made sure I walked around to keep myself healthy. Each passing month had become harder, and now that I was entering my third trimester, it felt like it had been years since I'd seen my cunt.

Not Harrison, though. He ensured I always felt sexy and wanted and took good care of me in that aspect as well — but he'd been going easy on me, and I needed my rough man sometimes.

When he got home from work, I could hear he was surprised to find Quentin downstairs with the kids, but seeing as he was between semesters, he had been stopping by often to hang out with them and be the "cool uncle."

I wasn't complaining, because that meant he was babysitting while I was upstairs naked under the sheet and ready to push Harrison until he gave me what I craved.

The second he entered the room, I grinned, slipping that sheet off of my body so he could see all of me. Predictably, my husband stripped his suit jacket off and climbed up on the bed with hungry eyes, taking a moment to rub my swollen ankles.

"Stunning, Briella. So… fucking stunning."

"Yeah? Should I get some photos taken like this?"

I imagined Harrison letting a cameraman into our house for that and chuckled, but I'd underestimated my man. "Yes. Tomorrow, I'll take them myself. You're cutting me off, after all."

I didn't have any complaints there. I hummed as he rubbed my skin, relaxing in seconds at his touch. "Twins have been moving so much today, they're finally sleeping."

"Good. And how is my good girl today?" he asked, kissing over my belly.

"Okay. Wet." I smiled innocently as he met my eyes, narrowing his own slightly.

"Oh?" His fingers trailed down my thigh to my pussy, flicking lightly through the mess there. "Bred and soaking wet… just how I love my beautiful little slut."

I twitched, missing how it felt when he spoke to me that way. "Yes, Sir. I showered this morning, and now your little slut needs your come. I'm empty without it."

"Can't have that," he tsked, spreading my legs further and leaning down to lick me.

I was permanently wet while pregnant with all of my kids, but Harrison still always took the time to take me apart with his tongue. Reaching down for his head was hard, so I gripped the sheets instead, groaning and arching in pleasure as he ate me like I was dinner. "God, I'll never get used to this... so fu-king good!"

He ate me like he loved the taste, loved the fact that he was licking the pussy that made him a father, like he was determined to make me come so I'd be more pliant.

The first wasn't enough.

The second wasn't enough.

Two fingers and a third orgasm were barely enough — but Harrison was done waiting. He finally came up for air, his beard a fucking mess, and I tugged him in closer and begged so he wouldn't take it easy on me. "Please! Please fuck me like I'm your dirty little slut."

"Bri, I—" his breathing hitched as he slid inside me, pushing in until his cock was so deep, it was almost uncomfortable. "Won't hurt you, Briella. Not like this."

"You won't. Please, baby. I miss being your little slut."

He rolled his hips hard and held me down. "Is there ever a time you're not my little slut? Just think about it, Briella. If you're not pregnant with my child, you're hanging off my cock so I can breed you again. Sounds like a little slut to me, hm?"

His thrusts got sharper, his dirty talk grabbing me by the clit and holding on strong. "Fuck! Yes, I'm your little slut. I'm your little sl—"

I came again, throbbing and pulsing as he pistoned into me, reaching up to grab my throat and squeeze.

"Good girl," he growled. "My beautiful, perfect, cock hungry little slut. So fucking wet... you want my come?"

"Yes! Come inside me, Sir. Mark up your dirty girl."

I lifted my legs so he could get deeper, whimpering with each rough thrust that did exactly what I needed them to do. I was too wet to feel him fill me up, but I felt his hand tighten around my neck, his fingers slip into my mouth to tug my jaw down, and sure as hell felt him spit on my tongue and shove my mouth closed again.

"Mine forever," he grunted. "Mine."

"Yours... only yours," I gasped, pleased I got my way once again... I always did with him. "I love you."

"I love you too. Now tell me five things you love about yourself."

He pulled out, dropping down to kiss my stomach lovingly as I struggled to focus on me. It was hard to think about yourself when you had small children that came first, but Harrison continuously ensured I did. "Um… I love my body when your babies are inside me, I love that I'm still your dirty little slut, I love the mother I turned out to be, and how we're raising our children. Um… how many was that? Oh, I love my ability to always get my way."

Harrison sighed at the last one, but there was nothing in his eyes but love. "Brat."

"Mmhm. But you love me. Come hold me and tell me how happy I make you."

"I can do that." He slid in behind me, pulling our bodies flush and wrapping a protective arm over my stomach. "Are you tired, beautiful?"

"Yes. You did all the work and I'm still exhausted. Your boys have been kicking every organ they can reach today."

"Our boys are strong, but you're stronger. Sleep, Briella. I'll clean you up once I hear you snoring."

It seemed like the best time to drop a bombshell on him, because there was no way he'd let me feel his wrath right then — though I probably should have warned Quentin to run first. "Okay. Oh, and I made the appointment for you to get snipped today. It's a week after the boys are due, but if they're anything like their siblings, they'll come a little early too. Night, baby."

Nothing but tense, complete silence greeted me, and I smiled to myself as I closed my eyes and settled in.

Harrison was going to spank the hell out of me when this was all over, and I couldn't fucking wait.

# The
## Snip Date

"Hey, you know what I just realized?" I walked over to where Harrison was laying with a playful grin. "Both of our crotches need a lawyer. What do you think? Personal injury? Wait no, property damage."

"Definitely property damage," he agreed, adjusting the frozen bag of peas he had nestled around his balls. "Still think this was cruel."

I pouted my lip at him sarcastically. "So does my vagina. Eye for an eye, or maybe eye isn't the right body part." I couldn't stay away even while teasing him, so I climbed on the bed and laid my head against his arm. "They'll be fine, Har. We have enough babies and you got plenty of recordings of me pregnant."

"I know. It's just… strange thinking that part of our life is over," he admitted. "No more buns."

That time, my pout was genuine. "I know, and I loved having your bun in my oven. But if we hadn't done this, we would have kept having kids until we were way too old because we both loved it too much. But every pregnancy was harder on me than the last. I don't think I can handle any more. I'm sorry it seems cruel, but you're welcome to still breed me all you want and we can pretend. I froze some of my milk for you."

He pulled me in to kiss me slowly. "I love you, Briella. You're right, they have gotten harder on you, and the last thing I want is to hurt you. I'll get over my loss of free-flowing sperm… as long as I still have you."

"You got me. You always will, and I'm excited for our future. It won't all be diaper changes and tantrums. They're already growing so fast."

"I still can't believe Arlo is five," he admitted. "Or that little Piper is about to be two. They'll all be in college before we know it."

"I know. Earlier today Arlo asked me if he has to marry Blaire because he doesn't want to."

I chuckled, curling happily into Harrison's arms as he pulled me in. "God, I hope not. Is he enjoying the dress Quentin got him?"

"Yes. He loves it, but he said he's not ready to wear it out of the house yet. He's also still firmly Team Boy for now, but I imagine he will let me know if that changes. He's still little, he'll figure out who he is in time."

Harrison kissed my temple. "He will. And if it ever comes to it, I'll get you a suit and me a dress and we'll take him out for ice cream. No one should ever have to hide who they are just to

make sure other people aren't uncomfortable."

My eyes watered, and whether it was
the hormones still running rampant
through my body or how sweet my
husband was, I wasn't sure, but my
children and I were lucky to have him.
"I love you. I just feel so angry when I
think of the children without a dad like
you."

"And yet, you cut me off," he
sighed. "Hypocrite."

"I cut you off after five of them,
Harrison. Five tiny humans that all
look up to you. How many more could
you have handled?"

He raised his brows. "Technically,
you cut me off after three. I bartered
for the fourth and lucked out with the
fifth. But honestly… no more. I want
you to myself again one day."

"Fucking lawyer," I muttered. "I'm
not so bad then. I want you to myself
too one day."

"I'm going to need at least forty-
eight hours before that day comes,

though. My balls feel like they're on fire right now, and having you this close to me is hard enough."

"Sorry for your balls. I'd kiss them, but I don't imagine it would help." I grabbed his hand and kissed his fingertips. "But maybe I'll make that up to you soon."

He grunted, shaking his head quickly as he pulled his hand back. "Don't. Fuck, Bri... I can't get a boner right now."

I sat up from the bed and gave him some room. "Okay, I'll go check on the kids. Twins went down not too long ago, so hopefully they sleep a bit. Keeping up with their appetites has been rough. Need anything from me, Sir?"

"More than I can ask of either one of us right now," he admitted. "Want you bent over my knee."

I pretended to slowly bend over, but stopped before I could drive him too crazy. "Raincheck, baby. You can punish me later."

# 11 DATES

I blew a kiss and dashed out before he could call me a devil woman and went to check on the kids. Luckily, the twins were still fast asleep, but I found the other three having a tea party in Piper's room and joined them. The tap water wasn't the greatest so I surprised them all with some lemonade instead and enjoyed the tiny smiles on their faces.

It was a moment I'd hoped I'd remember forever.

~

Now that Harrison was all healed, it was time for that punishment. It was something I'd been eager for since he promised me it was happening, so I slipped on some lace panties and stared at my body in the mirror. It had definitely changed over the years, but the way I felt before a scene hadn't, and this was a rush I wanted forever. "I'm ready, Sir."

## JENSEN

"God, you're gorgeous, Briella," he whispered, tugging me in and brushing his hands down my waist. I'd bounced back after Arlo and Blaire, but not so much after Piper... and the twins had ruined me. The stretch marks, the saggy skin, the extra pounds that were simply a part of me. "So fucking beautiful."

He built me up, running his strong, broad hands over my curves as he praised me and trailed his tongue over the stretch marks on my ass, then finally sat on the bed against the headboard and bent me over his knee before checking to see if I was comfortable.

My skin was on fire in a way I'd become addicted too, something Harrison always did to me. I nodded quickly to tell him I was good. "Green, Sir. Thank you."

"Good girl. Now breathe, and remind me how many of these you racked up during this last pregnancy."

I focused on the light taps and smooth circles he rubbed into my skin to warm it up, smiling to myself before I decided to make it worse. "Probably only like one."

"Hundred?" he asked. "One hundred? That sounds accurate. Open your mouth, Briella. You're going to suck my fingers for the first twenty, at least."

I opened for him and relaxed, letting him feel how ready I was for the punishment I'd earned.

The first few came quickly — just teasing, sharp little slaps that had me squirming, but weren't too bad. Most of my attention was on the way Harrison was finger-fucking my mouth, keeping me speared as he gripped my ass and shook it, spanking every few seconds.

It was exactly what I'd hoped it would be, subspace coming easily as he owned my body and helped me ride that line of pleasure and pain — that road between heaven and hell.

## JENSEN

One of my favorite places to be.

I drooled as he pulled my thighs apart a little further and spanked me harder. "Wet for me, Briella? Should I find out?" he asked, slipping two fingers inside my dripping pussy. "Mmhm… my beautiful little whore loves being punished, doesn't she?"

"Mmhm," I hummed, clenching around him to make him crave me even more.

"No coming, Briella. Just keep that in mind."

He fingered me hard, pulling out every few seconds to spank me then shoving those digits back in until I was screaming and fighting the urge to beg. Incoherent words dropped freely from my mouth as I rocked back on those fingers when he'd give them to me, but fuck, it was getting harder to focus.

*Thwack.*

"Bounce so pretty, Briella. Wish you could see how red your ass is right now."

*Thwack.*

I bit down softly to beg in my own way, making him hiss and smack my cheek.

"Brat. Count to ten. Now."

I did — or I tried. The numbers came out in drooly babbles as he spanked me hard, rapidly smacking down on my sore ass.

"Is this what you wanted when you teased me?" he asked, rubbing the skin for a moment before spanking me again, and again, and again. "Wanted to be bent over my knee like a bad girl?"

"Yes!" I grunted, white-knuckling the sheets with tears in my eyes. "Please!"

"My dirty little whore loves to be spanked. Bet you'd squirt for me if I gave you permission, hm?" he teased, hooking his fingers inside of me and slamming his palm against my raw skin. The fucking speed, the rough-ness, the relentlessness had me nod-ding desperately. "Please, Sir. Please let your little slut come. She'll be a good girl."

"Then come, Briella. Now."

His thumb pressed into my ass as his fingers brushed my g-spot over and over again, making me twitch and moan his name so loudly, I worried someone might hear, but I couldn't help it.

I squirted all over his hand, loving the way it made his cock throb and twitch under me. "Good girl," he growled. "Keep fucking going."

The next rough, sharp spank stole the breath from my lungs — his hand was soaked, restraint snapped, and he had me flipped onto my back before I could even blink.

Feeling his tongue was like a glorious torture I never wanted to end. I came so many times I lost count, lost track of everything but his tongue on me like a lifeline that tethered us together and kept me on Earth.

When he finally quit, I was boneless and half asleep, but I still felt every single kiss he placed to my skin — the ones over my ass where he'd spanked me, the inside of my thighs where he'd bit me, my cheek where he'd slapped me.

I could hear the praise ghosting between his lips about how beautiful I was, how good I was, how much he loved me.

How happy I made him.

Knowing that after all these years, after five kids and countless fights and sleepless nights, he still cherished me like this… it was how I knew we'd make it through anything. "I love you," I mumbled, clinging to him even though I didn't need to.

He wasn't going anywhere.

# The Holi-Date

## Harrison

When I was younger, I had very specific, vivid dreams of what my future would look like. Ten years before an earthquake forced me to admit how I felt about Briella, I knew — she was the one I wanted to spend my life with.

The one I wanted to build with, to grow with.

I couldn't explain it then, and I still couldn't explain it now. But somehow... I'd known the day she'd walked into my law firm that she was the love of my life.

So, I'd dreamed... dreamed of a happy wife, a dozen kids, a house big enough for all of us to be comfortable without being so big that we never saw each other. I dreamed of Sunday breakfasts and summer pool days and Super Bowl parties with my brothers, our friends, and good food.

I dreamed of the comfort my good girl would bring me after long days, after bad news, after the weight of a trial threatened to take me under. I dreamed of how life would change us — how my beard would turn grey, her once-sharp edges would soften.

I dreamed of a love so strong it brought me to my knees... and I got it.

All of it... and some matching Christmas pajamas, too.

I frowned down at them, then met Briella's mischievous gaze. "Seriously?"

"Yup," she said excitedly. "I finally found some for all of us that arrived on time. You're matching your beautiful family."

## JENSEN

She pouted her lip for good measure, making my heart skip a beat like it always had. "Okay, brat." I pulled her in for a slow kiss, brushing my nose against hers. "The butt flaps are a nice choice. It'll make it easier for me to bend you over and take you once our kids are all in cookie comas."

"That's what I'd hoped for." We could hear the twins bickering about who was taller, but we ignored them, taking a moment to stare into each other's eyes. "I told your brothers they all have to wear pajamas too. It's a rule or they can't come in."

I snorted at the thought, but kissed her all the harder for it. "Brilliant, sassy Briella. You never cease to surprise me."

That held true after we got changed, as well. When I'd gone to sleep, we had the tree up and a few random decorations here and there — I'd been working a lot of late nights, Arlo was always off somewhere, the twins had sports, and the girls just didn't seem to care enough — and while I'd tried to be fine with it, Briella knew me, and knew exactly how much Christmas meant to my family.

And now the entire first floor was covered in decorations.

"How?" I asked, taking in the lights lining every wall, every bookcase. "When?"

"Last night. Arlo and Blaire helped the most, but… all of us worked together. I wanted to surprise you."

My chest tightened. "Every time I think I couldn't love you any more, you prove me wrong. Thank you, beautiful girl."

I wrapped her in my arms and just held her, breathing in the scent of her messy hair and soaking in the warmth radiating off of her.

"You're welcome. We also made cookies yesterday that we're all decorating as a family. Arlo!" she yelled, and the second he poked his head out from his room, she lowered her voice. "Can you put on the Christmas music? The playlist we made."

"Yeah, let me hook up to the speakers. Should I just put it on repeat for the day?" Bri looked way too excited as she nodded and he smiled at us. "Nice PJs, dad. I wasn't sure she'd convince you."

I clicked my tongue. "You're almost sixteen. Let's not pretend like you haven't been around long enough to know I'm utterly incapable of saying no to your mother."

That only made him smile wider. "It's what she deserves." He shrugged like it was common knowledge as he synced up to the speakers and started looking around for food. "Is everyone bringing a… partner or something?"

My eyes narrowed slightly. "Just the ones you know about. Why? Did you invite someone?"

"No," he rushed out. "I was just curious. I'll go change."

He left the room quickly and Bri chuckled. "He's been hanging out with someone, I just don't think he's ready to introduce him yet."

"Hm. I'll keep that in mind on New Year's," I promised, heading for the door when one of my brothers knocked.

A half hour later, my living room was so full that I couldn't move at all — but seeing Roman in a onesie with a butt flap was worth it.

Oh god, was it worth it.

I snapped about a hundred pictures to blackmail him later, then donned my Santa hat to pass out gifts once everyone found a spot to sit in and settled down. It took a while for everyone to get their pile of presents with how many of us there were, but when it was time to dig in, the room was filled with the sound of ripping paper and happy chatter.

The eggnog in my glass helped loosen me up just enough to play a little song on piano once all the presents were opened, and it was there, in that moment, that I knew all my dreams had come true.

I may not have had a dozen kids with Briella, but I had five of my own and enough nieces and nephews to nearly make up the difference — and at the end of the day, it had been this feeling I'd been chasing, anyway.

Fulfillment, love, contentment.

Happiness.

It was enough to have me bickering playfully with Roscoe and Edison as they tried to convince me which one of them was cooler. "Well, Ed sucks at basketball. I'm pretty good, Dad. Like the best in my class," Ros argued.

"Nuh uh!" Ed yelled. "I am!"

"And what if I said Piper could beat you both?" I asked.

They scoffed, banding together in their own defense. "Piper's so wrapped up in her best friend Jackie, she wouldn't even try."

"Shut up, Roscoe. You're just jealous I have friends, and Dad's right. I can beat you both."

Ed grabbed her to put her in a headlock. "Only because you're taller than us right now. Give it a year, Pip-squeak. We'll kick your as—"

"Edison!" I snapped, glaring daggers at Roman when he started cackling. "It's Christmas."

"He was going to say we'll kick your antlers. Right, Ed?"

Arlo rolled his eyes at his siblings. "You three are ridiculous. We all know Blaire can kick all our asses in everything."

I sighed, rubbing my beard as I considered cutting them all out of my will. "Okay. I want you to go around and tell each of your siblings your favorite thing about them, and the next one of you who even considers cussing in my presence is getting a swirly."

Arlo snapped his jaw shut like he hadn't realized he'd cussed. "Sorry, Dad. Uh… I like Blaire's glasses, Piper's creativity, Edison draws well and Ros plays the guitar better than Uncle Q."

"Bullsh— oot," Quentin argued. "Pretty dang close, though."

"Hence why you were always second fiddle, Q." Roman winked, then kicked back with his fingers laced behind his head. "I'm kidding. He's better than me, most of the time… but maybe that's because he's sober more often."

I opened my mouth to change the conversation yet again, but my kids beat me to it. They followed Arlo's lead and paid each other compliments until all five of them were blushing and looking away from each other like the awkward little shits they were — which was exactly what I wanted.

"Perfect," I said. "Time for the yearly family Christmas photo, now that you're all embarrassed and docile. Bunch up."

Blaire rushed over to get the camera and set up the tripod as we got into place, and once she settled in and pressed the button, I just had to hope everyone was smiling. Either way, there was always Photoshop.

"Wait, one more!" Piper yelled. "Everyone make a funny face."

The chaos that ensued after as my kids tried to make their cousins laugh nearly sent everyone toppling to the ground, but the laughter was... beautiful. We were buried in torn wrapping paper, empty boxes and discarded bows, but I'd never felt so much love in one room before, and I wasn't sure I ever would again.

It had me drinking in every second, cherishing every moment before my brothers took their leave, our twins went to bed, the girls disappeared with Briella upstairs, and Arlo sat down next to me on the couch to stare at the tree.

"Another successful Christmas?" I asked him.

He nodded with a soft smile on his lips. "I'd say so, for sure. Did you get everything you wanted?"

"I always do. The hair dye someone put in my stocking was a little rude, but that's fair," I teased. "I'm not that grey."

Arlo looked at my hair and bit back a laugh. "It was Uncle Ethan. Isn't he older than you? Maybe we should get him some diapers next year."

"Maybe we should." I eyed my oldest with a curiosity I was barely biting back — but if he wanted me to know he was hanging out with a boy, he'd tell me on his own, and I wouldn't betray his confidence with his mother by telling him I knew. "Did you get everything you wanted?"

His deep brown eyes dropped, his tell that he *did,* in fact, want to talk about something he wasn't sure how to approach. "Not quite. Do you remember when we went to get ice cream when I was little? You wore a dress with me."

"Yes, and your mother proved she looked better in a three piece than I ever could. I still have the dress, though. Why do you ask?"

"Well, I don't really wear those any-more, but… I also don't want to wear the boxers I got for Christmas. Is it okay if I go shopping for my own underwear soon?"

Of all the conversations I didn't expect to have, this was at least in the top ten — but I was honestly just relieved he wasn't asking for condoms yet. "Of course. If you have a specific store in mind, I can take you in a couple of days."

He blushed, nodding as he turned back toward the tree. "So you never minded? That I didn't like a lot of boy things?"

"Arlo, you've been perfect since the day you were conceived. It never mattered to me at all what you liked to play with or wear. You're my first born… I was honestly just glad you were human, healthy, and not a figment of my imagination. Have you ever doubted that?" I asked gently, knowing I'd tried hard over the years to make all of my kids feel accepted for who they were, but I wasn't flawless.

He shook his head. "No. But my b— my boyfriend's parents feel differently. I don't get it. He's their first born too, y'know? Why not just love him?"

"Because some people are just… unhappy," I said, knowing it didn't come close to excusing the homophobia in our world. "But you tell your boyfriend that if he ever needs a place to stay or a hug from supportive parents, our door is open, okay?"

I could see the grin on his handsome face even though he was still trying to hide from me. "Thanks, Dad. You think there are more cookies? I don't know what Mom put in them, but I swear they get better every year."

"Should be. Go grab a couple and then get your antlers up to bed." I stood to help him off the couch, then pulled him into a hug. "Merry Christmas, Arlo."

"Merry Christmas, Dad." He squeezed a little tighter than normal, and I realized with a jolt that we hadn't hugged like that in a while. With as distant as my own father had been, I made a mental note to do better moving forward and kissed the top of his head before sending him on his way.

For a few moments after that, I took in the living room, the mess, the lights, the tree, and the fire fading to nothing in the fireplace, then shut everything off to go upstairs and find my wife.

She was braiding her hair in the mirror, still wearing the pajamas she made us all wear, but her ass flap was open for me. "Hello, Sir."

"God, you make those look good." I slid behind her, touching over her hips and kissing her neck. "Thank you, Briella."

"For… leaving my ass on display?" She smiled, baring her neck for more. "Or for something else?"

"For being you, for giving me five incredible children, and for making reality better than dreams," I said, biting gently and touching her curves. "I'm so fucking in love with you, kitten."

Her smile widened at the pet name. "I'm in love with you too, Harrison. So deeply in love it consumes me sometimes. Thank you for our children, for our lives, for choosing me when you could have chosen someone who wasn't a brat."

I chuckled, playfully nipping her shoulder. "My life would've been boring if I had. I needed you," I admitted, sweeping her off her feet to carry her to bed.

The truth was that I'd always need her, no matter how much time passed — and I wouldn't change a single thing about my good girl, my beautiful Briella… my wife.

I couldn't imagine anyone luckier than me.

# The Moving Date

I soaked in the bathtub with bubbles all around me and my husband behind me. He was rubbing soothing circles along my shoulders, comforting me after one of the hardest days of my life — we'd moved into a smaller home and said goodbye to the twins as we sent them off to college.

Every single one of my babies had left the nest, and it was such a bittersweet milestone that I was struggling to find the "sweet." I already missed them all, missed the bickering, the noise, the moments we all sat around the dinner table with a board game in front of us.

They weren't over, I knew that, but without them living here, I didn't have the luxury of calling them all down-stairs and forcing them to have family time. We'd have to coordinate around busy schedules or wait until a holiday, and worst of all, my babies would be facing all the trials and tribulations of adulthood without me by their side.

There were positives, though. Our children were raised with love and ac-ceptance, things the outside world needed more of, and sending them out into it was good for our society.

Not to mention, Harrison and I would have much more time for this... for us. "Our home is quiet."

"First time in almost twenty-five years," he agreed, rubbing my shoul-ders just the way I liked. "Feels strange."

"I know. I remember the moments where I couldn't wait to have you all to myself again, and now that it's here...

I miss them. Think we'll ever stop worrying about them?"

"Not a chance, but they're strong, Briella. Just like their mother." His lips brushed my head. "And now, I can go back to spoiling you every day. I wasn't quite done yet when Arlo came along."

I hummed, more than happy to hear it. "That helps. I want to do a scene, Sir. I want to forget how worried I am about those kids, forget everything but you and how to breathe. I need it more than I've needed it in a long time."

"Do you have anything specific in mind?" he asked gently. "Tell me what you need, kitten. I've got you."

I took my time responding, loving the fact that he wasn't rushing me to choose. It was hard. We'd done so many scenes together over the years that it was almost impossible to pick exactly which one I needed in that moment. I was seconds away from begging him to pick for me, to take that off my shoulders too, but instead, it came to me. "Can we role play? Maybe bring out those old masquerade masks from the closet and pretend we just met? We can put on some music downstairs and dress up. We have the whole house to ourselves. Let's make the living room a dance floor and put drinks on the counter. Let's remember how it felt the very first time we met."

"Of course. Sex, or no? We both know that bit took us a decade and a natural disaster," he chuckled.

"Yes, sex. Rough sex. Take me how you wanted to the day we met. The way you should've."

His eyes darkened in the way that I loved. "I can do that. And your safe-word, kitten?"

"Blizzard, Sir. Though I haven't felt cold in a very long time."

"Good girl... always my good girl."

I felt better as we finished up my bath, and by the time I was climbing out of it, I was excited.

Our fire was still burning strong, and deep down, I knew it would never go out.

# 11 DATES

~

Once the house was all set up with candles, drinks, finger foods and soft music, we parted ways to go get dressed, and I went with a simple, shimmering purple dress that matched my mask then went downstairs to wait by our makeshift bar.

My heartbeat sped up when I saw him. He was wearing the tux he married me in with a jet-black tie, his hair slicked back, and that mask covering just enough of his face to give him an air of danger and mystery.

He was still as stunning to me at this age as he always had been, and the small, flirty smile he flashed toward me as the music started had familiar butterflies scattering around in my stomach.

I was happy I never got used to those.

I brought my drink to my lips and broke eye contact to see how he would have reacted if this really were the night we met, and he didn't disappoint me. My heart pounded harder as he stalked closer, staying just out of reach but close enough to hear over the low thrum of the music — and something about the promise in his raspy voice was sending shivers down my spine.

"Are you here all alone, kitten?"

"Yes," I responded simply. "Are you?"

"I am." He stepped in closer, gently spinning me and pulling our bodies flush. Feeling him pressed against my back was grounding, a gentle reminder that I belonged to him.

"Not anymore. What's your name, handsome?"

"Harrison," he muttered, ghosting his lips along the side of my head as his hands slid around my body. "And who might you be?"

"Briella Lewis. I just moved here," I hummed, melting into his touch and reaching back to touch his neck.

His teeth caught my earlobe. "And

do you always dance so seductively, or is this just for me?"

"Hmmm…" I pretended to ponder. "I might always dance this way, especially when I'm this horny."

"Pretty little slut like you won't have to be horny for long," he promised, teasing the hem of my dress and dancing his fingertips over my stomach. "Surely you'll find someone to fill your greedy little holes soon."

I couldn't stop the small moan from escaping my lips — his touch, his words, *all* of him was enough to have me soaking wet and nearly regretting my choice not to wear underwear.

But as his fingers dipped lower, just grazing my pussy, I knew that I'd made the right choice.

"Bet you'd let me take you right here, hm? Wouldn't even need to find a bathroom. All I'd have to do is tell you to get on your knees and you would."

I gasped. "Yes, Sir. Right… here."

My legs clenched together as I bit my tongue, but Harrison wasn't having any of it. He smacked my clit and roughly shoved his hand between my thighs to spread them apart again as he growled low in my ear, "Bad girl."

The fact that my knees didn't give out was a miracle. "Do you want me to be your good girl?"

"I do. Get on your knees, Briella. Open that pretty fucking mouth for me."

Dropping down felt like a reward. I floated straight into subspace as my knees hit the hardwood floor and I let my head fall back as I opened my mouth.

"So eager," he praised, slowly undoing his belt. "Want my cock, beautiful girl? Show me that tongue."

I rolled my tongue for him, salivating as he pulled out that beautiful cock — the same cock I'd been fucking and sucking for nearly twenty-five years, the one that bred me and gave me our wonderful life. "Yes," I gasped breathlessly, emotions bubbling under my skin. "Please let me have it, Sir."

"So fucking beautiful," he whispered, stroking himself and smacking my lips with the head. "Lift that dress of yours, Briella. Touch that pretty pussy while I use your mouth."

I complied, loving how deep he was breathing as he watched me rub my clit and lick his cock. He forced my lips apart and sheathed himself in my mouth with a rough, quick roll of his hips, then tugged the mask off my face to see my eyes better and fisted a hand in my hair.

"Be a good little slut and open your throat."

I groaned as he slid deeper, vibrating his cock as I pressed harder on my throbbing clit. This was exactly what I wanted, no… exactly what I'd needed.

"Good girl," he breathed, holding steady with his cock buried completely in my throat. "Make yourself come just like this. Show me what a dirty little slut you are."

It wasn't hard. All I had to do was allow myself to live in that moment and feel nothing but pleasure and Harrison. I was coming within a minute, dripping down my fingers as I choked on him and struggled to breathe.

I was still his good little slut.

"Fuck. You do it, kitten? Get your hand all wet for me and stroke my cock."

My hand was already soaked as I brought it up to stroke him, eyes locked on his gorgeous green irises as he lost control and fucked my fist.

"God damnit, Briella," he hissed. "Get up and bend over."

My stomach was filled with pesky butterflies once again as I stood, bending over right there for him to see my glistening cunt under my dress.

"So wet for me," he growled, slapping my ass and dragging the tip of his cock through my folds. "Tell me you need it, little slut. Tell me you need a fat cock splitting you open."

"Oh fuck me, I need it. Please, Sir. I'll die without your cock. Need to feel you split me open… breed me… ruin me for anyone else."

Strong hands braced me as he slid inside me, bending me over in the middle of the damn living room. "You're mine, kitten. This pussy is mine."

"Yours. Only yours," I braced my hands on my knees as he rocked deeper, groaning at the unbalanced feeling that had me sitting back on his cock to bottom out. "Oh god, you fill me so good."

"Don't I? Almost like your pussy was made for me."

One sharp thrust nearly had me toppling forward, but Harrison's hand wrapped around my throat to keep me in place and make me take every inch until I was coming again, this time squirting all over his cock and down my thighs. "Fuck me!" I groaned. "Show me who I belong to. Fill me up like the dirty little slut I am."

His other hand wrapped around my throat too until I was speared on that cock, back bowing as he drove himself deeper inside of me. "Should've known you liked that," he grunted out. "Being marked inside and out, used like a whore. Take it then, kitten… fucking… take it."

He slammed against my ass, grinding hard as he emptied inside of me, and even with how heavy the day was before this, I'd never felt lighter.

Somehow, one scene like we used to have lifted that weight off my chest and brought me right back to the place I'd always loved — the place I knew I was safe.

Harrison Stag's mercy.

"Briella," he whispered, pulling me up to kiss my skin and fuck his come a little deeper. "My good girl. My beautiful Bri."

"Your good girl," I repeated. "Tell me five things you love about me, Sir. Please."

"Only five? I… love your sense of humor, how strong you are, how familiar your body is to me after all these years," Harrison answered. "I love your

**145**

heart, and what a brilliant, wonderful mother you are."

Happy, unshed tears filled my eyes and I basked in those words, in the security blanket that was my husband. "I love the small frown between your eyebrows when you're grouchy, how sexy your hands look as you do mundane things around our home, the life you've given me with those gorgeous balls and your amazing mind. I love the father you are so much it makes me cry, makes me feel like I'm the luckiest woman in the world. I love you. All of you."

He kissed up the column of my neck to my cheek, then nuzzled in to breathe in my scent. "All mine, Briella. I can't wait to grow even older with you. Thank you for always being my good girl."

I would be, because even when I was his bad girl, I would still always be his good girl. Maybe that didn't make sense to some, but it didn't need to.

This was our life… and we intended on living it.

# Want more of the Stag brothers?

Check out Ethan Stag's book, *Sin Sessions,* available October 11, 2022:

Trapped in a failing, sexless marriage, I sought the help of a highly-recommended therapist in hopes he'd help me find my spark again.

It was the perfect plan until I actually set foot in his office. Dr. Ethan Stag was sinfully hot, everything I'd ever wanted, and grooming me to be his good girl whether I knew it or not.

He wasn't saving my marriage at all.

He was saving me.

## Also By
## Octavia Jensen

**BOYS OF BRISLEY:**
King Hunt
Exposed King

**ELEVEN:**
11 Hours
11 Scenes
11 Dates
Sin Sessions

**WHITECREST:**
Business & Pleasure
Eyes On Me
Can't You See
Over A Cliff
Motocross My Heart
Rose-Colored Boy

**STANDALONES:**
Don't Go
With All My Broken Pieces

**BLACKRIDGE:**
Take Me Twice

# VISIT OCTAVIA JENSEN AT

www.celiketchpublishing.com/
octaviajensen
Or check her out on social media!

**Facebook**: Author Octavia Jensen
**Instagram**: @authoroctaviajensen
**TikTok**: @authoroctaviajensen

Printed in Great Britain
by Amazon

85789038R00089